THE HARE
AND THE TORTOISE

To my sporty Lil'
Love Mum
L.K.

For Keith,

ISBN 978 1 40830 960 5 (hardback)
ISBN 978 1 40830 968 1 (paperback)

Text © Lou Kuenzler 2011
Illustrations © Jill Newton 2011

The rights of Lou Kuenzler to be identified as the author and
Jill Newton to be identified as the illustrator of this work
has been asserted by them in accordance
with the Copyright, Designs and Patents Act, 1988.

A CIP catalogue record for this book is available
from the British Library.

1 3 5 7 9 10 8 6 4 2 (hardback)
1 3 5 7 9 10 8 6 4 2 (paperback)

Printed in Great Britain

Orchard Books is a division of Hachette Children's Books,
an Hachette UK company.

THE HARE
AND THE TORTOISE

Written by Lou Kuenzler
Illustrated by Jill Newton

ORCHARD

Old Aesop lived long, long ago.
(He was an Ancient Greek, you know.)
The many fables that he spun
are always wise and often fun.

His moral tales give us advice
reminding us we must be nice.

Be very good to Mum and Dad.
Don't EVER make your teachers mad.
Don't tell a lie. Don't play a trick.
Don't gobble sweets until you're sick!
Please pay attention to these words
Unless you are a pack of nerds!

This awesome fable you might know –
the hare was fast, the tortoise slow.
Hare was fit and sleek and thin:

He drank a shake at every meal
to make his muscles strong as steel.

The bubbling drink was pretty grim.
Hare always put some odd things in:

Add six worms to badger poo,

mix and grind them to a goo.

Brew a cup of fungus tea,

drizzle over weasel pee.

The tortoise always tried his best,
but didn't even own a vest,
or trainers, or those skimpy shorts.
He wasn't very fond of sports!

Hare would laugh and tease old Torty,
all because he wasn't sporty!

His steps are slow and very small.
He doesn't seem to move at all.
He doesn't stretch and strain and groan.
I think he must be made of STONE.

He never tries
 to leap or jump —
just plods along,
 the lazy lump!

11

Tortoise slipped inside his shell.
Why couldn't Hare get lost as well?

Big Ears had loads of sporty mates.
So why not go and lift some weights –
with Gary his gorilla friend,
or find some iron bars to bend?

Why not wrestle hefty foes,
like Crazy Rex, the big rhino?

Or Jeremy, the kangaroo —
he was good at jujitsu.

So Torty hid, quiet and still,

He tried his best to shut Hare out.
But Hare behaved just like a lout!

He threw the shell up like a ball
and catching it began to call,

15

Hare peered inside where Tortoise hid . . .

The tortoise wasn't keen to bet.
He didn't want to run or sweat.
It would be mad to join the race –
the hare would set a fiendish pace . . .

The tortoise had a sense of pride.
He took a moment to decide,
then poked his head outside the shell,

Hare laughed as if his guts would burst,

But it was done. The time was set.
They'd meet next day to seal the bet.
It was too late for turning back.
A rope was strung around the track.
Stalls sprung up with souvenirs –
hats, balloons and ginger beers.

You couldn't miss Hare's loyal mates –
they all sped in on roller skates.
Whippets, zebras and a cheetah
cheered for Hare with a loud-speaker!

Hare is sure to win the bet!
Hare Force one – he's like a jet!

Slugs and snails soon joined the crowd.
They cheered for Tortoise extra loud.

Koala bears and sloths came too.
They called themselves:
THE TORTOISE CREW!

Torty shuffled proudly past,

I'll do this thing! I won't be last!
I'll win this race for all us folk . . .
Cos, being slow, it ain't no joke!

Yet when the starting whistle blew
Hare leapt forward – he almost flew.

The tortoise whispered very low:

We'll see, my friend . . . but off you go!

START

A penguin with a microphone
broadcast the race for those at home:

This pair is really very funny –
an ancient tortoise and a bunny!
The hare has sped off up the hill.
But Tortoise is just standing still.

Hare's already hit his groove,
While Tortoise barely seems to move.
Athletic Hare is very fast.
Pathetic Tortoise will come last!
A snail could beat this shuffling pace.
Hare must, by now, have won the race!
This really is a hare-brained scheme –
the silliest race I've ever seen!

The penguin raised his microphone:

This race is done – Hare's on his own!

And he was right to think that way.
The leader was ten miles away.
Hare had surely won the race!
Tort would end up in disgrace.

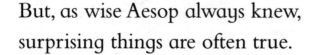

But, as wise Aesop always knew,
surprising things are often true.

Though Hare had
   run off at full tilt,
he soon began to
   tire and wilt.
His blistered feet
   were red and raw.
But Torty's toes
   weren't even sore.

While stinky Hare
   was dripping sweat,
Tort was as cool as
   fresh courgette!

We shouldn't laugh – it isn't funny –
but Hare was now a hot cross bunny!
He spied a shady tree ahead –
it looked like such a tempting bed.
A cool and breezy place to lie
and let his sweaty armpits dry!

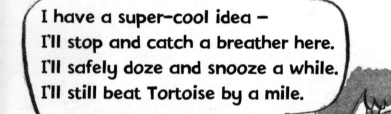

I have a super-cool idea –
I'll stop and catch a breather here.
I'll safely doze and snooze a while.
I'll still beat Tortoise by a mile.

Hare was sure he'd won the race.

That ancient stone can't beat my pace!

He lay down for
a power nap ...
and fell asleep –
Zzzz! – just like that!

Hours later, at long last
(for Tortoise really wasn't fast),
Tort shuffled round the final bend.
And there he saw his sleeping friend.

He did not give the hare a shake,
or call him so that he would wake.
He just went plodding slowly past:

**Perhaps, my friend
I won't be last!
I know you think
I am a rock —
but you may be
in for a shock!**

Hare snored LOUDLY in his sleep!
He didn't hear the slightest peep.

As Tortoise shuffled by unseen,
The hare was lost inside a dream.
In his dream, Hare was the best –
a number **1** upon his vest!

35

Dreamy Hare was sleeping still
as Tortoise climbed the final hill.
And as the crowd began to shriek
Hare was woken from his sleep.

Now half awake, Hare rubbed his eyes . . .
Could that be Tortoise near the prize?

Hare pinched himself, but was awake.

He leapt towards the finish line
But knew at once he'd left no time.

Hare sprinted at his fastest pace...
But, with one step, Tort won the race!
The crowd went wild with WHOOPS
   and CHEERS:

Tortoise bowed and felt quite chuffed.
He wasn't even slightly puffed.

He gave a winner's interview
to Penguin's television crew:

I'd like to thank
my mum and dad,
cos being slow
isn't always bad!

Hopping mad, in wild distress,
Hare called to Penguin and the press,

But Tortoise proved his win was fair.
He showed the crowd his feet were bare.

Hare's eyes filled up with angry tears.
He wiped them off with his long ears.

I know how hard
   Tort must have tried.
I lost that race
   through my own pride!
I'm beaten by
   a walking stone!
I've had enough!
   I'm going home!

But Tort called kindly after him,

Let's meet tomorrow . . .
at the gym!

He'd won the race and now he thought
he might just do a bit more sport.

That's it, folks. We've had our fun.
This Aesop's fable is all done!
Thanks to Tortoise and to Hare,
there is a moral we can share:

It's often found to be the case,
that **SLOW AND STEADY WINS THE RACE!**

AESOP'S AWESOME RHYMES

Written by **Lou Kuenzler**
Illustrated by **Jill Newton**

All priced at £4.99

Orchard Books are available
from all good bookshops,or can
be ordered from our website,
www.orchardbooks.co.uk,
or telephone 01235 827702,
or fax 01235 827703.